Busy School

written by Melanie Joyce
illustrated by Sue King

Ladybird

It's a busy day at Busy School.
The playground's very noisy.
Everyone runs about.

But Cilla waits with her mum.
Is there something the matter?

It's Cilla's first day at Busy School.
She's feeling very nervous.
"Be good," says Mum.
"And remember, have fun."

But Cilla is really shy.
Do you think she'll be all right?

Miss Miller does.
She's really nice.
"It's all right, Cilla," she says.
"Everyone gets first day nerves.
We'll soon have you settled in."
And she does.

Cilla sits with Annie and Viv.
They smile and say, 'hello'.

Miss Miller calls out the register.
Then it's time to make a start.
What will the class do first?

First they do some counting.
1, 2, 3, 4, 5...
Miss Miller points at pictures.
The class counts them out loud.

They count the numbers on the clock.
It's nearly time for playtime!

After playtime there's a story,
about Jack and a big beanstalk.
Miss Miller reads it out.

Everyone listens carefully.
They love the scary giant.
Especially noisy Freddy!

"Quiet now, Freddy," says
Miss Miller.
"We're going to do movement.
Imagine you're a big beanstalk,
and stretch up to the clouds."

But what is Freddy doing?

"I'm the scary giant," he roars.
He *GRROWLS!* in Cilla's ear.
Miss Miller says,
"You can be the giant,
but please don't frighten Cilla."

Freddy says sorry and pretends
to be a quiet scary giant.

At lunchtime they go to the dining hall.
There's lots of noise and clattering things.

Everyone talks at once.
Especially Cilla and her new
friends.

After lunch it's painting class.
It's Cilla's favourite bit.
She gets some brushes and lots
of paint.

What is Cilla painting?

It's a great big roaring scary giant.
Miss Miller thinks it's good.
And when Freddy comes to look
at it, Cilla *GROWLS* and makes
him jump.

Everyone laughs. Even Freddy.

It has been a busy day at
Busy School.
But Cilla is really happy.
She says goodbye to Miss Miller,
and runs to meet her mum.

Cilla's not nervous any more.
She loves her new school.